THE PSYCHO IN HIS STORY WAS ALIVE!

"Take the top letter and pass the rest back," Mr. Glabrous said. "No fair picking a pen pal by his country. And I want you to use your very best handwriting. Consider yourselves foreign ambassadors."

B. B. took her letter and handed the stack to Jason. "Here you go," she said.

The tips of Jason's fingers burned when he touched the top envelope. The school's name and address were typed by a laser printer. But there wasn't any return address. And no postmark. The stamp wasn't even canceled.

Jason sucked in his breath and tore into his envelope. He pulled out a piece of computer paper. The edge of the page was dark brown and curled, as if it had been burned.

Jason squinted at the words jumping off the page:

Dear Jason—

Discarded

I can help you win the short story contest. But first you gotta get me outta your computer.

Your pen pal,
Blowtorch

Read these other **BONE CHILLERS** from HarperPaperbacks:

BONE CHILLERS

BLOWTORCH@ PSYCHO.COM

Created by
BETSY HAYNES

Written by
SHERRY SHAHAN

HarperPaperbacks
A Division of HarperCollins*Publishers*

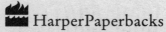 HarperPaperbacks

A Division of HarperCollins*Publishers*

10 East 53rd Street, New York, N.Y. 10022-5299

This is a work of fiction. The characters, incidents, and
dialogues are products of the author's imagination and are not to
be construed as real. Any resemblance to actual events or
persons, living or dead, is entirely coincidental.

ISBN 0-06-106450-5

HarperCollins®, 🔥®, and HarperPaperbacks™
are trademarks of HarperCollins*Publishers* Inc.

Cover art © 1997 Daniel Weiss Associates, Inc.

First printing: July 1997

Printed in the United States of America

Visit HarperPaperbacks on the World Wide Web at
http://www.harpercollins.com/paperbacks

❖ 10 9 8 7 6 5 4 3 2 1

For Vicki León: an uppity girl-fiend

Chapter

Jason Reed chewed off a dirty hangnail and spit it out onto the floor. It wasn't really dirt. Just a glob of dried peanut butter left over from lunch. He checked the nails on his other hand, looking for a smear of jelly.

What would he have if he laced his fingers together? A peanut butter and jelly *handwich*. Jason chuckled at his joke.

He slumped down in his chair and stared at the words on the computer screen. Checking for food under his fingernails was something he did when he was thinking. At the moment he was concentrating on the plot of his latest short story, "Blowtorch Burns Buns."

Now his fingernails clicked across the keyboard. *Creepy crook*. No, he'd used that on a different page. What about *super-duper bad dude?* Yeah, that was more creative. He had to be creative if he wanted to grab the judge's attention.

The deadline for Edgar Allan Poe Middle School's annual short story contest was two weeks away. For the first time in the history of the contest, the top fifteen stories would be published in a book. A real book with a hard cover and black-and-white illustrations inside.

Jason had dreamed of being a famous thriller writer ever since he could remember. He gobbled up flesh-tingling novels the way most kids devoured junk food. Most of his friends had posters of rock stars and sports dudes on their bedroom walls. Jason's walls were papered with jumbo photocopies of book jackets.

Even his parents joked about it. "Your first words weren't mama or dada. They were Stephen King."

Sure enough, an autographed picture of the king of horror stood on Jason's nightstand.

Last week Jason's best friend, Cambria Pines, had bought him a used copy of *How to Write Chiller Thrillers,* by J. Jimjam. Cambria was also entering the contest, but her story was about a star skateboarder. And she'd probably never finish it. All her spare time was spent at the skateboard park doing "research."

Jason was undoubtedly the only kid in school who spent weekends working on his story. It had taken two whole days just to outline the plot on a legal pad. The main character, Blowtorch, was a burly prison inmate locked away for life. The charge? Murder in the first degree.

Blowtorch had dropped a high-voltage hair dryer into the guy's Jacuzzi. That's what gave Jason the idea for the title.

There weren't any witnesses. No fingerprints. An untraceable murder weapon. At least that's what Blowtorch thought. Actually the hair dryer had been bought by his mother through a mail-order company. UPS delivery instantly traced it to Blowtorch's address.

Jason loved thinking up gross physical features to give his main character. Blowtorch had a crusty scab under his left eye from last week's riot in the mess hall. The reason for the riot? The cook had added canned peas to the steamed carrots. A smushy mess. Both Jason and Torch hated cooked peas.

The how-to book said all characters should be

well-rounded. Even bad dudes had to have a weakness. Otherwise they wouldn't seem like real people. So Jason gave Blowtorch a few food allergies. Beans, especially chili beans, gave him gas so bad, his stomach inflated like a beach ball. Grated Swiss cheese and cooked onions, which reminded Blowtorch of maggots, made his scars wiggle as if they were alive.

"Huh?" Jason jumped, startled by a knock on his door. That happened sometimes. He would be so involved in a story, he'd forget where he was.

His dad came in, carrying a dinner plate. He was a secretary in a law firm, and he always wore a crisp white dress shirt and colorful suspenders. His medium-long hair was slicked back, unlike Jason's buzz, a cut so short his scalp had a suntan. Jason had his dad's freckles, which were the same color as cocoa after the marshmallows melted.

"Mom thought you needed a healthy snack," his dad said, smiling at Jason over the top of the plate. "To keep the creative juices flowing." He set down the snack and leaned over the computer. "How's the story going?"

"No fair peeking," Jason grunted, then slapped his hands over the screen. "You have to wait until I'm done."

"Okay, okay," his dad said lightly. Snapping his suspenders, he headed toward the hall. "But I want an autographed copy of the book when it's published."

Jason swiveled in his chair and glanced at all the book jackets on the walls. Maybe he'd have a jumbo photocopy made of the book of short stories. Sure, why not? His name along with the names of the other contest winners would be printed on the cover.

He could see it now: Jason Reed, in bold letters, raised and shiny black.

Jason's computer and printer fit on a built-in desk wedged between two closets across from his bed. The doors had been taken off one of the closets, and the opening now held bookshelves. He had arranged his collection of Stephen King novels in alphabetical order.

Did his dad say "autographed" book? Wow! Would people really want his autograph? He needed to work on his handwriting. It was much too neat. Autographs should look like scribbles.

Yeah, this was going to be a great year. It was a leap year. And since Jason was born thirteen years ago on February 29, most of his birthdays were celebrated one day early, on February 28.

Lucky thirteen, he thought. *I bet my parents have something extra-special planned.*

Four years ago, on his last "leap" birthday, his parents had taken him and a bunch of his friends to the fair. The kids had stuffed themselves with mustard-slathered corn dogs and wads of cotton candy. Then they went on all the twirly rides. What a blast!

Jason turned back to his snack. On the plate was something that resembled a burrito. At least it was a flour tortilla. Brown stuff oozed out of both ends.

It didn't look like anything he wanted to *touch*—let alone eat. And it smelled like burning rubber.

But since his mom had gone to the trouble to make it, he decided to examine it more closely. Unrolling the outer layer, he stared at the stuff inside. Chili beans with melted Swiss cheese.

"No way!" he gasped, flinging the mess back onto the plate. "Blowtorch's allergies!"

Was this some kind of joke? But how? Jason had never said a word about Blowtorch or his allergies. So his mom didn't know about them. Was it a coincidence?

"Yeah, that must be it," he muttered to himself. "A big coincidence."

Then he spied something shiny in the beans. He leaned in for a closer look. His eyes widened. *Cooked onions?* His mom knew he hated cooked onions. They were soft and slithery like worms. She never put the slimy things in his food. *What's going on?*

Chapter

2

Jason tried to use logic to explain away the bean burrito. A humongous coincidence? Maybe. More likely he had mentioned Blowtorch and his weird allergies to his parents and then forgotten. Sometimes when he was in the middle of writing a story, he was absent-minded.

Or maybe he had started talking in his sleep. Hadn't he read somewhere that sleepwalking and talking was something that happened to teenagers? And his thirteenth birthday was less than a week away.

Jason switched off the computer, stood up, and stretched.

It was time for a short break. Tomorrow was Monday, and he hadn't done any homework. *I should at least do my math work sheet,* he thought as he dragged his backpack onto his unmade bed.

He was in the middle of the first math problem when he heard a knock on the door.

Cambria didn't wait for an answer before pushing into his room. "Do you want to go to the park?" she asked, smacking her gum.

Cambria was wearing her new BoardStiff skateboard T-shirt. Bright purple pads covered her knees and elbows. She swung her helmet by its strap. Jason knew her skateboard was parked on the front porch.

"Eee-uu. What's that?" she asked, wincing at the brown burrito. "Someone have an accident?"

Jason shook his head. "Mom's idea of a healthy snack."

"Healthy snack?" She laughed. "Those words don't belong in the same sentence."

Jason laughed, too. He considered telling her about the burrito—that it was made from the same stuff as Blowtorch's allergies—but he decided against it. It suddenly seemed stupid to think it was more than a coincidence.

"Grab your skateboard," Cambria said, smoothing her copper-colored curls under her baseball cap. "Let's go."

Jason glanced at the computer and mounds of notes scattered around the desk. "Guess I could work on my story later," he said. "Blowtorch won't mind if I go to the skateboard park for a while."

"Blowtorch?" she asked, glancing out the window. "Who's that?"

Suddenly the computer screen turned primrose pink. It was the same color as the hair dryer at the crime scene. Sparks flew off the screen and landed on Jason's notes—threatening to burn them to a crisp.

Jason slapped at the paper. But small holes had already burned black dots into the sheets on top. "Did you see that?" he asked, wide-eyed.

"What?" she said casually, turning from the window.

"What do you mean, *what?* The computer . . . the screen . . ." He waved the singed paper as evidence. ". . . the sparks."

"It's okay if you want to work on your story instead of going to the park." Cambria punctuated her remark by popping her gum. "All you have to do is say so."

"The computer must have a glitch," he said, thinking aloud. "Maybe it's about to crash. Or maybe there was a power surge in the neighborhood. Either way, I'd better print out the last scene. Go on without me."

"A bunch of parents are building a jumping ramp—I can't wait to try it." Cambria swiveled on her paisley-patterned sneakers. "Try to come over later, okay?"

Jason nodded without answering. With the contest only two weeks away, a meltdown was all he needed. He punched a few keys, commanding the computer to print the last draft.

"Come on," he muttered impatiently. "Hurry up."

The printer started spitting out pages. Jason quickly reread the scene that showed Blowtorch bribing a guard with cold hard cash. In exchange Blowtorch could have a prison computer in his cell.

According to the latest outline, Blowtorch would use the computer to tap into the prison library system and work on his appeal. His strategy? Blowtorch planned to frame his mom for the hair-dryer murder.

Jason glanced at the pages. "Hey? What's going on?"

He read them over again. But the words remained the same. Instead of using the computer for research, Blowtorch had tapped into a program called Pen Pal.

"That was the first draft of my story." Jason stared unblinking at the paper. "I deleted those pages last week."

Jason flipped through the yellow pad that held his new outline just to make sure. "See?" He shoved his notes at the computer as if the screen could read. "No Pen Pal program."

Jason slumped in his chair. Did he forget to dump the first draft? Did he forget to enter the new version? No way. He shook his head. He might be a bit scatterbrained, but he wasn't crazy.

Jason highlighted the section about Pen Pal and hit *delete*. Nothing happened. The words stared at him from the screen as if challenging him. He highlighted the same section and dragged it to the trash can. He hit *dump trash* and waited. Still nothing.

Now what? he wondered. He couldn't think of anything else to do except turn off the computer. No *save* or *shut down*. He just flicked the switch and watched the screen blacken. But before it darkened completely, the word *HELP!* flashed in 48-point letters in italics. Jason never used italics. J. Jimjam had written in his book *How to Write Chiller Thrillers* that editors hated the squiggly letters.

Jason backed slowly away from the computer,

half expecting it to start up again. *Ridiculous.* But the computer acted like it had a mind of its own. Either that or someone was messing with it. Who? Certainly not his parents.

There was only one other possibility: Blowtorch.

The idea was so frightening, he pushed it out of his mind. Jason plopped down on his bed and turned his attention to the math work sheet. It was in the form of a crossword puzzle, thirteen squares linked together in a long chain.

The answers to the math problems matched up with a list of letters that fit into the squares. Jason wondered what the squares would spell when they were filled in. He quickly figured out the first letter, *I.* And there were three *N*s.

Jason didn't realize he'd drifted off to sleep until he felt his mom's hand on his shoulder. "Jason, wake up," she was saying. "It's time for dinner."

Jason stretched, causing his notebook to fall to the floor. He glanced at his mom, whose hair was almost as short as his buzz but dyed the color of Concord grapes. "What're we having?" he asked through a yawn.

"Homemade chili." Then she rubbed his buzz. "But you don't have to worry about gas, Fuzzy Wuzzy."

Jason hated being called Fuzzy Wuzzy. It was a nickname some of the kids at school had used when he first got his buzz. Others had called him snaggle brain. His parents never called him names. *Never.*

"No gas for Fuzzy," she repeated. "I bought a bottle of Bean-o Cuisin-o. It's a scientific and social breakthrough that stops gas before it starts."

His mom handed him the bottle before leaving his room. Jason was reading the label when a flesh-tingling shriek threatened to shatter his eardrums. It sounded like his mom had stuck her hand in the garbage disposal.

"Mom?" Jason cried, then jumped off his bed and scrambled down the hall.

Chapter

3

Jason's heart skipped a beat when he heard another alarming shriek. "Mom?" He stubbed his toe on his desk and realized he wasn't even in the hall. He was still in his bedroom and half asleep.

The Bean-o Cuisin-o conversation had been nothing but a dream. A *bad* dream. He should've known. His mom never called him Fuzzy Wuzzy.

Jason limped down the hall. His mom sagged against the doorjamb leading to the bathroom. Her face was drained to the color of raw onions. The screams *hadn't* been a dream.

"What's wrong?" Jason asked, following her gaze.

His dad teetered shakily over the pedestal

sink. Blood was splattered everywhere, dotting the shiny white porcelain and tile backsplash. A few sticky drops clung to the mirror.

"Razor slipped." His dad smoothed a Band-Aid over his cheekbone. "You know how razor cuts bleed. Jeez, you'd think I'd been sliced with a chain saw."

"That's not funny," said his mom.

Jason squinted at the morning sunlight filtering through the high window above the bathtub. It spotlighted the bloody splotches.

I must've nodded off doing my homework, he thought. *And my parents decided to let me sleep.*

His mom pulled an old handkerchief from the pocket of her overalls. "Let me mop this up," she said, wiping the sink.

Three mornings a week she drove a garbage truck for the local dump company. Overalls helped keep coffee grounds and soggy diapers at arm's length. Disposable diapers, she'd said often, were clogging the landfill.

The front of his dad's crisp white shirt was red polka dot. "Do you want me to get a clean shirt?" Jason asked him.

"I'll get it," said his mom.

Jason slowly stepped into the bathroom. The

cloth Band-Aid was the same width and length as Blowtorch's scab. The cloth strip was even the same burnt brown color. And it was in the same place.

How could Dad cut himself that close to his eye by shaving? Jason wondered. *Beards don't grow up that high on the cheekbone.*

Jason plopped down on the toilet lid to think about it. Taped to the tank was a boldly printed sign: If It's Yellow, Let It Mellow. If It's Brown, Flush It Down. One of his mom's ideas to conserve water.

His mom returned a few minutes later with a clean shirt. "The rest of your white shirts are at the cleaners." She held up a shirt with light blue stripes set against a beige background. Pinstripes. *Prison* pinstripes. The same shirt Blowtorch and the other inmates wore.

Jason jumped up. "Dad has a zillion white shirts," he heard himself screech, but he couldn't help it. "They can't all be at the cleaners!"

"I don't mind wearing stripes for a change," said his dad.

"But you always wear a white shirt to work." Jason stomped his foot for emphasis. "*Always.* And suspenders!" At least his dad still wore his

17

usual suspenders. Miniature scales of justice were stamped into the design.

"It's an attack of low blood sugar," said his mom, as if that explained her son's behavior. "We should've woken him last night for dinner. The bean burrito just wasn't enough."

Low blood sugar? Jason wondered. *What does that mean?*

Jason decided not to mention the burrito. It was fertilizing the flower bed under his windowsill.

"Let's have some breakfast." His mom placed her hands on Jason's shoulders and guided him to the kitchen. She eased him into his usual spot at the table. "What kind of cereal do you want?" she asked. "Hot or cold? With or without bananas?"

Jason mumbled, "I don't care." His head whirled as he thought about all the weird stuff that was happening. Everything had to do with his short story for the writing contest and Blowtorch.

"Mom's right," his dad said, heading to the coffeepot. "We should've woken you for dinner. But we thought you needed the sleep. You've been working so hard on your story."

His dad always drank coffee from his

favorite Legal Eagle mug. He'd gotten it as a gift from the law firm on Secretary's Day. But this morning he poured his coffee into a tin cup.

"Where's your mug?" Jason asked. "The one with the eagle?"

"It broke," his dad said flatly.

"It broke?" Jason repeated.

The two words had a frightening ring.

Then his mom set a bowl on the kitchen table—a metal bowl with matching utensils. "I'll get the cereal," she said.

Jason leapt to his feet. His chair crashed over backward. "Where are the regular dishes?" he demanded, opening the cupboard above the dishwasher.

A complete twelve-place setting of tin dishes and bowls with matching cups and saucers filled the space. Yesterday the shelves had held stoneware dishes with a sunflower pattern.

Jason tore through the drawers, looking for the silverware with the yellow enamel handles. "What happened to the silverware?" Nothing but plain metal utensils remained, all with dull edges.

"What's wrong?" his dad asked.

"Calm down," his mom added.

Jason swung open the pantry doors. The

19

shelves that usually held an assortment of canned goods were stuffed with canned beans. Beans. Nothing but beans.

"If you don't want cereal this morning," said his mom, "I can whip up an omelet."

"That sounds good," his dad said. "Do we have any Swiss cheese?"

"A Swiss cheese omelet." His mom smacked her lips. "How does that sound, Jason?"

Jason didn't answer. He raced to the den and grabbed the cordless phone. Then he crouched in a ball under the desk.

"Jason?" his mom's voice tracked him down the hall. "Where are you, Fuzzy Wuzzy?"

Jason punched in Cambria's number. "Come on," he begged into the receiver. "Answer the phone." A busy signal answered him.

"Fuzzy Wuzzy? Are we playing a game?"

Jason felt himself break out in a cold sweat. He pressed redial and waited. Still busy.

"Jason?" Now his dad joined in the search. "It's time for breakfast, son."

Yeah, right, Jason thought. A Swiss cheese omelet. With cooked onions? And beans on the side?

On the third try Cambria answered the phone. "Hello?"

Chapter

"Sure," Cambria had said when Jason asked her to meet him before school. "Where?" Then she'd tossed in, "What's wrong with your voice? You have a sore throat or something?"

"I'm whispering," he'd strained before hanging up.

Escaping from his parents wasn't too difficult. He used the same path as the bean burrito: out the bedroom window. Now he waited anxiously for Cambria on the corner of Spark and Pyre Streets, their usual meeting spot in front of the fire station.

Where would he start? With Blowtorch? But how could a character take over a story? And how could that same character take over his parents? It didn't seem possible.

Jason spotted Cambria whizzing down the

street on her skateboard. Her purple knee and elbow pads were in place. And her wild curls were tied up in a ponytail.

Jason glanced at his baggy surfer shorts, wrinkled all the way to the knees. His T-shirt was worse, as crinkled as crepe paper. He looked like he'd slept in his clothes, all right.

Did I remember to brush my teeth? he wondered. The only Shakespeare quote he'd memorized popped into his head, "The rankest compound of villainous smell that ever offended nostril."

"Do you have any gum?" he called to Cambria.

Cambria stopped with a three-sixty spin. "That's why you asked me to meet you? Because you wanted a piece of gum?"

Halitosis, Jason had to admit, was the least of his worries.

He shifted his weight from one high-topped sneaker to the other. "We've been friends a long time, right?"

Cambria looked at him funny. "Best friends for almost a year. Why did you ask that? Is something wrong?"

Part of his brain was yelling, *Spit it out!*

Another part was saying, *She's going to think you've cracked up!*

His whole body shook as if the two sides were fighting it out. "Something strange is going on at my house," he began slowly. It was suddenly more important than ever that Cambria believe him. "And when I tell you, I don't want you to think I'm a space cadet."

"I won't." Cambria's expression was suddenly as serious as his tone. "I promise."

"It's about my story—"

"The one for the school contest?"

"Yeah." Now more than his hands were sweaty. "You're not going to believe this, Cambria, but I think my main character—" He was interrupted before he could say, *My main character has taken over the story. And he's taken over my parents, too.*

Stupid Barbara Burton rushed across the street. She waved her arms like she was flagging down a freight train. "Hey, guys!" oozed a sickeningly sweet voice. "Wait up!"

Jason groaned. "Oh, no." He couldn't stand Barbara Burton, nicknamed B. B. She was always bugging him.

B. B. had had a crush on him since the fourth grade. Now they were in seventh grade. That meant he'd suffered through three years of her gooey-eyed stares. It was practically a lifetime.

To make things worse, B. B. sat in front of him in English class. She was always passing dumb notes over her shoulder. Notes written on pink paper with little fairies in the margins. Gross!

Jason didn't hate girls—after all, Cambria was a girl, and she was his best friend—but B. B. was a serious contender for a hate list, if he ever made up one.

B. B.'s best friend, Angela Robb, tagged along with her. Angela was just as disgusting. She wore her retainer around her neck. It dangled from a chain intended to hold sunglasses. Everyone knew the reason. Angela's mom always asked Angela if she wore her retainer at school. And Angela always answered yes without lying.

"How come you're going to school this way?" B. B. asked Jason.

"Yeah, how come?" Angela mimicked.

Cambria rolled her eyes in disgust.

Jason stared at B. B. How did she know the route he took to school? What did she do? Follow him?

I have to get rid of them, he told himself. *Both of them. And fast!*

"Um, I had trouble with the math homework. Cambria is helping me with the puzzle part," he said. "Go on ahead of us, okay? Or we'll all be late for school."

"I got an A-plus in math," said B. B., slipping her long blond hair over her shoulder. "Why don't you let me help you?"

"What answer did you get to the crossword puzzle?" Cambria put in. "I bet it's not the same as mine."

B. B. knelt on the sidewalk and started rummaging through her backpack. Her binder and books were quickly scattered on the sidewalk. "If it's not the same," she said, "then yours is wrong."

Cambria must have known B. B. would fall for the trick. "See ya!" Cambria called over her shoulder, then pushed off on her skateboard.

"The answer is incineration!" B. B. shouted after them.

But Jason and Cambria didn't slow down until they reached the grassy field on the edge of Edgar Allen Poe Middle School. A bunch of other kids arrived at the same time, some on bikes, others on in-line skates.

Jason stared at the bike rack. Today he was about the only kid without a set of wheels.

"Okay," Cambria said, fitting her skateboard sideways into the rack. "What's going on?"

Jason stopped to catch his breath. Everything that had happened this morning was so unbelievable. Had his dad really switched to pinstripe shirts? Had his mom really bought metal plates and eating utensils? What about the razor cut? And the pantry filled with canned beans?

"Jason?"

Jason's mouth was as dry as a peanut butter sandwich. Maybe it had been a dream. Or maybe it was his imagination. The book Cambria had given him had a whole chapter about novel writers and their overactive imaginations.

"Jason?" Cambria nudged him. "What is it?"

Jason cleared his throat and started at the beginning. His sentences were as choppy as the water in the Jacuzzi at the murder scene. "Prison riot . . . razor blade . . . and chili beans, lots of gross brown beans . . ."

"Beans?" Cambria stared at him like she was tired of playing this stupid game. "What're you talking about?" she demanded.

Chapter

The first bell of the day rang, and the scream of slamming lockers filled the corridors. Everyone hustled to their first-period class before the tardy bell rang.

Cambria and Jason stood in the hall outside their English class. A group of kids pushed by, chattering about a new TV show.

"This is a joke, right?" Cambria said, but she wasn't laughing. "Knock, knock. Who's there? April. April who? April Fools'! Only Jason, this is February, remember?"

How could he forget? His birthday was only a few days away.

"So what gives?" she asked with a playful punch.

Jason sighed loudly. Now that he'd spit it

out—put the whole crazy story into words—that's exactly how it sounded, like a joke.

"I'm not kidding," he said. "And I can prove it."

"How?"

"Can you come over after school? I'll let you type some stuff into the computer," he said. "Then you'll see that Blowtorch won't let you save it. Or he'll twist your words into something different."

"I'll come over," Cambria agreed. "But I bet there's a logical explanation for everything. Your computer probably has a glitch."

"What about my parents? They were acting really weird."

Cambria rolled her eyes as if to say, *All parents are weird*.

But she said, "Maybe they're planning a camping trip for your birthday. And your mom wanted to try the metal bowls ahead of time."

That sounded reasonable. "But what about my dad's shirt?"

"So he wore a striped shirt? Instead of a white one?" she asked. "What's the big deal?"

"And six shelves of canned beans?"

Cambria just shrugged.

A few more kids hurried into the classroom. Now Mr. Glabrous, the English teacher, filled the doorway. The principal had given Mr. Glabrous special permission to wear a baseball cap in class because of his hair-pulling problem.

The disorder even had a name: trichotillomania. Last week Mr. Glabrous had given it as a bonus vocabulary word. The "Dear Gabby" column in the school newspaper even talked about the disorder. It said there were twenty-five million people in the United States who couldn't stop pulling out their hair. And there was no known cure.

Jason thought Mr. Glabrous had something to do with the column since the English teacher was the newspaper's editor. The column even printed the address of the Trichotillomania Learning Center in case someone wanted more information.

"Come on in," Mr. Glabrous said. Today's cap said, All Bald People Look Good in Hats. "The tardy bell's about to ring."

Jason and Cambria followed Mr. Glabrous inside. Jason's seat was in the middle row, halfway down the aisle. Cambria was all the way in back by the pencil sharpener.

Jason snickered at the empty chair in front of him. B. B. was probably still stuffing her books in her backpack. It was bad enough that she sat in front of him. But she was constantly spinning around in her chair and making gooey eyes at him.

"Yuck," he groaned as B. B. skidded into the room a split second before the bell rang. Today her socks matched her short plaid skirt. Even her hair clip was covered with the same plaid material. B. B. always looked like she stepped out of a mail-order catalog.

Angela flew in next, her retainer bobbing against her chest.

Mr. Glabrous called the class to order and took a quick roll. "Here!" and "Yo!" bounced around the room.

Jason jumped, startled at the sound of his name. "Jason?" Mr. Glabrous called.

"Huh?" Jason blinked.

"It looks like you're here," said Mr. Glabrous. "At least there's a familiar-looking boy in your chair."

Twenty-six students roared with laughter.

"Oh, sorry," Jason stammered. "I mean, here."

Jason's mind was still on his short story. Cambria's explanation about the new bowls and silverware sounded logical. And Cambria was right—his dad wearing a striped shirt wasn't that big of a deal. She might've offered equally logical reasons for the other stuff—his mom calling him Fuzzy Wuzzy, for instance—if Mr. Glabrous hadn't interrupted them.

Jason sagged in his chair and breathed easily. For the first time in two days he felt himself starting to relax.

Mr. Glabrous was jabbering on about a new English project. He held up a stack of envelopes, all shapes, colors, and sizes. "The first batch of letters from our pen pals arrived yesterday," he said. "Two letters came all the way from Nairobi. That's the capital of a country in Africa called Kenya. Isn't that exciting?"

At the words *pen pal* Jason felt the gooseflesh rise on his arms. Even the light blond arm hairs stood at attention. "Pen pals?" he whispered across the aisle to Logan Lantz. Had he been absent when Mr. Glabrous first talked about the project?

"What pen pals?" Jason asked.

Logan was drawing a black widow spider on his hand. He added a poisonous red spot with a marker. "Beats me," he said, sniffling.

Logan was always a mess. Today he wore two different sneakers, both with missing laces.

B. B. swiveled in her chair and dropped a

31

note on his desk. "This is for you," she said in her usual flirtatious tone.

The note was written in purple ink: *Will you be my pen pal? Love, B. B.* A string of Xs and Os filled the margins.

Jason huffed a bored sigh and wadded it up. Spit wad material. B. B. took the hint and turned around again.

"Take the top letter and pass the rest back," Mr. Glabrous said. "No fair picking a pen pal by his country. As soon as everyone has an envelope we can start answering our letters. And I want you to use your very best handwriting. Consider yourselves foreign ambassadors."

All the girls squealed as they opened letters from New Zealand, Puerto Rico, and Turkey. The guys mostly grunted, "Cool!" and, "All right!" as they ripped into their envelopes.

Cambria waved an envelope postmarked Guatemala. "I wonder if it's written in Spanish."

"Are you going to grade our letters?" Angela called out.

"No way," Logan said, wiping his runny nose on his sleeve. "Reading someone's mail is a federal offense."

"Yeah," Ryan added. "You can get arrested for that."

"They might even call in the FBI," said Logan. "Since the letters are from other countries."

Mr. Glabrous calmed the class with a wave of his hand. "That's enough."

B. B. took her letter and handed the stack to Jason. "Here you go," she said through fluttering eyelashes.

Jason ignored her.

The tips of his fingers burned when he touched the top envelope. The school's name and address was typed by a laser printer. But there wasn't any return address. And no postmark. The stamp wasn't even canceled.

"Did everyone get a letter?" Mr. Glabrous asked.

"I didn't!" Michael Webb shouted from the back of the room.

Jason jumped up and waved his envelope. "Michael can have mine!"

Mr. Glabrous strolled down the aisle. "Thank you for the offer, Jason. But he can have mine."

It was no use. Jason sucked in his breath and tore into his envelope. He pulled out a piece of computer paper. The edge of the page was dark brown and curled, as if it had been burned.

Jason squinted at the words jumping off the page:

Dear Jason—

I can help you win the short story contest. But first you gotta get me outta here.

Your pen pal,
Blowtorch

Chapter

Little electric stars danced in front of Jason's eyes. He felt sick to his stomach. Barfo sick. Ten times worse than tossing up hot dogs and cotton candy on a carnival ride.

"I have to show my letter to Cambria," he muttered to himself. "Then she'll believe me that something weird is going on."

He considered going to the pencil sharpener and dropping the letter on Cambria's desk. But Mr. Glabrous was wise to that note-passing trick. Besides, the room was too quiet to leave his seat. All the kids were writing letters to their pen pals.

The minutes clicked off as the clock's hand inched toward the end of class. Jason counted forty-five clicks before the bell finally rang. "Psst! Cambria! Dump alert!"

That was their secret code for *Meet me at the recycling bins.* Everyone else in school stayed away from the recycling quad. Jason kind of liked the smell of garbage. It reminded him of his mom.

"Two emergencies in one day?" she said in front of the container marked Can It. "That's a record."

But Jason didn't have time for small talk. "We can't wait till after school," he said. "We have to go to my house now."

Cambria stared at him as though his elevator didn't go all the way to the top. "You mean, cut school? We can't do that, Jason. It's an automatic suspension."

"I know, but—" Jason waved the letter at her. "Just read this. Then you'll understand."

Cambria unfolded the letter.

Jason waited, holding his breath.

"Will you be my pen pal? Love, B. B." Cambria burst out laughing. "Your pen pal is B. B.?"

"No, that's the wrong letter!" He stared at the scrolled purple writing. "I must've gotten them mixed up—the other one is still in my desk!"

"Calm down," Cambria said, "before you pop a hormone."

"Wait here," he said, swiveling on his sneakers. "I'll be right back."

A few minutes later Jason was pounding on the door of his English class. "Mr. Glabrous?" he called. "Are you in there?"

"Jason, my boy." His teacher's voice filtered out. "I've been waiting for you."

"Really?" Jason asked, stepping inside.

Maybe Jason had dropped his letter on the floor. Yeah, that was probably it. Mr. Glabrous had found it and was saving it for him.

Inside the room Jason had to pinch his nose. The smell of gas was overwhelming.

Mr. Glabrous hunkered over a sloppy pile of brown stuff on his desk. He was gobbling a bean burrito. Swiss cheese and onions oozed out both ends. The mess saturating papers on Mr. Glabrous's desk told Jason his teacher had eaten more than one of the bean concoctions. No wonder the room smelled like it did.

Scribbled on the chalkboard behind Mr. Glabrous was a recipe: Blowtorch's Bean Burritos. Jason wasn't surprised that Swiss cheese was the first ingredient.

"You're eating lunch?" Jason asked. His eyes were as wide and round as flour tortillas. "At nine o'clock in the morning?"

Mr. Glabrous smacked his lips loudly. Then he scooped a burrito onto a metal plate. "Not lunch," he said, licking his fingers. "Just a little snack."

Jason recognized the spotted blue pattern on the plates. It was the same pattern that was on his mom's new set of metal dishes.

"Would you like a bean burrito?" Mr. Glabrous asked, holding up the plate. "It's a gas!"

Then he laughed—a bone-jarring laugh that echoed around the room.

Chapter

7

Jason didn't tell Cambria he'd seen Mr. Glabrous inhaling bean burritos. *No, he thought. I'll wait until Cambria types something into the computer. Then when she sees Blowtorch twisting the words around, I'll tell her about the other stuff.*

Now that he thought about it, why would Blowtorch want people to eat those burritos? Chili beans was one of Blowtorch's allergies. It didn't make sense.

Jason considered another possibility. Could it be? Did Blowtorch want everyone else to eat the beans? To wipe them off the face of the planet? So he wouldn't have to eat them?

It wasn't easy convincing Cambria to cut class. "Suspension city," she kept saying.

"What about lunch period?" he tried.

"That's still a week's worth of detention if we get caught," she told him. "And sneaking off campus isn't the hard part. It's coming back."

"Yeah, all those hall monitors with whistles."

Jason was thinking about begging when she said, "Oh, all right. If it's that important to you."

Now Jason was pulling the house key from under the mat on the porch. The mat said, I Worship the Ground You Walk On. But Please Don't Track It into the House.

Cambria followed Jason down the hall to his room. Scraps of notes and old copies of his story littered the floor. It looked more like a landfill than a bedroom.

Jason slid into the chair at his desk. "Wait'll you see this." He turned on the computer and clicked on "Blowtorch Burns Buns." Then he scrolled to the scene that showed Blowtorch entering data into his computer.

"In my story Blowtorch uses his computer to tap into the prison library system," Jason explained. Cambria leaned over his shoulder, eyeing the screen. "He's suppose to be working on his appeal."

"So?" she huffed through cocoa rice crinkles breath.

"Blowtorch changed it all around. Instead of trying to frame his mother for the murder, he's in a program called Pen Pal. Get it? Pen Pal? Just like in English class."

Cambria scooted over a chair. "Come on, Jason. That's just a coincidence. A character can't change a story. It's not like he's real or anything."

"Oh, yeah? Just wait."

The words on the screen showed Blowtorch in his cell, hunkered studiously over his computer. He was surrounded by thick volumes of law books and was wearing wire-rimmed reading glasses.

"Hey!" said Jason. "What's going on?"

"What do you mean, *what?*" she asked.

"He's working on his appeal. Just like he's supposed to be."

Cambria raised an eyebrow. "Jason? Have you been getting enough sleep lately?"

"No. I mean, yes." Jason slowly shook his head to unscramble his brain. "You type in something. Then try to save it. Blowtorch will change it all around. Go ahead and try it. You'll see."

"What do you want me to say?"

"Anything."

Cambria sighed. She giggled, and her fingers clicked across the keyboard. *Roses are red. Violets are blue. B. B. the brat has a crush on you!*

"Very funny," said Jason. "Now quit and try to save it."

Cambria clicked on *quit.* The screen flashed, *Save changes before quitting?* She clicked *yes.*

Jason stared at the computer. "Hurry up," he muttered.

Jason hated waiting. It was like waiting for a teacher to call your name to give an oral report. Then she called someone else's name, and you had to wait all over again. Nothing was worse than waiting.

Finally the screen blackened.

"Okay," he said, "start it up again."

More waiting.

"Lunch period will be over in twenty minutes," she said, glancing at her watch. "And I can't be late for health class. I'm in charge of the happy hormone display, and I still have to fill the water balloons."

"Water balloons?"

"It's how I'm illustrating growth," she said. "With different amounts of water."

"Just wait until you see what happens, okay?"

The screen lit up.

Jason sucked in a deep breath. Then he punched up his story. Blowtorch was still hunkered over his computer. Still working on his appeal.

Jason read the words on his screen. "Roses are red. Violets are blue . . . no!"

Cambria rolled her eyes. "This isn't funny anymore, Jason," she said. "We cut lunch for nothing—now we have to sneak back into school. If we get caught, we'll get detention after school for a week. And I'll miss the wheelie demo at the skateboard park."

Jason was speechless, staring blankly at the screen.

He finally blurted, "But there's more!"

Jason dragged her down the hall to the kitchen. "The plates . . . knives . . . forks." He knew he was babbling, but he couldn't help it. "All metal . . . and the silverware . . . all dull."

The bottle of Bean-o Cuisin-o had vanished from the tabletop. The sugar bowl stood in its place. The dishwasher door was open. It was stacked with their normal dishes.

Jason yanked wildly on the cupboard door and snatched a plate—a ceramic plate with sunflowers. Then he tore into the silverware drawer. The slots were filled with yellow-handled knives and forks.

Frantically Jason raced to the bathroom. "They couldn't have scrubbed away all the blood!" he wailed. "There has to be blood somewhere."

Everything in the bathroom was spotless—as if Mr. Clean had swirled through the room with a magic wand.

Cambria looked inside the bathroom. "You've been spending too much time on your story," she said, glancing around. "You need to take a break. Maybe write some poetry for a change."

But Jason wasn't listening. He was bending into the clothes hamper, tossing underwear over his shoulder.

"Where's the bloody shirt?" he cried.

Suddenly Jason heard the front door slam. A voice called, "Jason? Are you home?"

Chapter

"**M**om?" Jason's voice echoed inside the clothes hamper.

"Um, Mrs. Reed," Cambria called out. "Hi!"

Jason's mom appeared in the bathroom doorway in her work uniform. Overalls and heavy work boots. Her face was smudged with something pea green. A piece of orange peel stuck to her cap.

"What're you kids doing home?" she asked, washing up in the bathroom sink.

Since Jason wasn't a very good liar, this was a tricky question to answer. *Think fast,* he told himself, closing the hamper lid.

"I needed something for school," he said. It wasn't much of a lie. His short story was a school project.

His mom took off her overalls and cap and dropped them into the clothes hamper. Underneath she wore shorts and a funky hot pink T-shirt.

Jason wondered, *Did she wash a load of clothes this morning? With the blood-splattered shirt? No, Dad's white shirts always go to the cleaners. So where is it?*

"Have you kids had lunch?" his mom asked.

Jason and Cambria answered at the same time. Jason said, "Yes." Cambria said, "No." They trailed his mom down the hall to the kitchen.

His mom didn't seem to notice the opposite answers. She set a large plastic bag on the counter. Then she started pulling things out to show the kids. "I can't believe people don't recycle this stuff," she said, holding up an aluminum tray from a TV dinner. Next came dented soda cans and a couple of squashed cardboard egg cartons.

Jason looked at his mom. She seemed normal enough. Nothing like she had been this morning. And she didn't call him Fuzzy Wuzzy.

His mom sorted the rest of the stuff into recyclable piles. "Why don't I fix a little lunch," she said, turning to the refrigerator. "Then I'll drive you back to school."

"That sounds great, Mrs. Reed," Cambria said. "And could you please write us a note? We aren't supposed to leave school during lunch."

"No problem," she replied, searching through the dairy drawer.

Jason watched his mom grab a block of Swiss cheese, then she opened the vegetable bin. *Onions?* he wondered. *Oh, please. Pick up an onion! Then Cambria will have to believe me!*

Just as quickly she traded the Swiss cheese for a jar of low-fat mayonnaise. "How does tuna on homemade whole wheat bread sound? With alfalfa sprouts?"

Cambria was already folding paper napkins into triangles. "Super."

"Jason?" his mom asked, slicing the bread. "What do you want to do for your birthday this year? We should plan something extra special since it's leap year."

Jason sneaked a sideways glance at his mom. February 29 was only a few days away. His mom never waited until the last minute to make plans for his birthday.

Mom has something up her sleeve, he decided. Maybe another trip to the state fair like last year. Or maybe a day at the circus. Posters for a three-ring circus were tacked up all over town.

"Surprise me," he said, playing along. But he secretly hoped it was the circus. The posters showed a dude doing backward flips on a motorcycle.

"Cambria?" his mom said. "Can you join us this Saturday? For Jason's birthday?"

Cambria munched on a stray sprout. "You bet."

While his mom and Cambria finished fixing lunch, he dashed to his room to check the computer one last time. If Blowtorch was still working on his appeal, just as he was supposed to—then Jason would have to admit that he, Jason Reed, was a mental case. Totally bonkers. Off the deep end. Or as one of Blowtorch's legal books would say, *Non compos mentis*.

Jason sucked in enough air to snuff one hundred candles, then he turned on the computer.

Chapter

J ason slouched in the backseat of the family van. Cambria and his mom were in front, singing with an old song on the radio. "They're coming to take you away, ho-ho, ha-ha, tee-hee. To the funny farm . . . "

The drive back to school is taking forever, he thought. *And it's only a ten-minute trip.*

Finally the van eased to a stop in front of the administration building. Cambria jumped out first. "Thanks for the ride, Mrs. Reed," she called. "And for the note."

"Yeah." Jason crawled out next. "Thanks, Mom."

Jason watched the van pull away from the curb. "Maybe *I* should move to a funny farm."

Cambria headed toward the monitor guarding

the front hall. "You were just overly involved with your main character," she said. "That's why your story is guaranteed to be one of the top-ten winners. Maybe even the grand-prize winner. Just wait and see."

Then she poked him playfully. "I haven't written one word of my story yet. Not even the title."

Jason tried to return her smile. "Yeah, you're probably right."

Over the next several days Jason convinced himself everything had been a hallucination. Except for one thing. His English class still smelled like gas. One of the kids had propped open the window. Another kid had pinched his nose with a large paper clip.

Mr. Glabrous had started wearing khaki-colored pants and bright pinstripe shirts. The same uniform worn by Blowtorch and the other inmates.

Jason ignored it.

A figment of my imagination, he told himself.

Jason even started losing interest in his story. Now that Blowtorch was working on his appeal, the story was sort of boring. It was sad, but true. If Jason was bored, would the judges be bored, too?

Maybe I should rewrite the ending, he

thought the next afternoon while he was staring at the computer screen. How about a prison breakout?

Jason pictured it in his mind: helicopters hovering over the prison, blinding spotlights fanning the block walls. Sirens wailing and guards armed with tear-gas bombs.

And Blowtorch? Nowhere to be seen.

It would be a flawless escape—Blowtorch crawling on his belly through the heating ducts.

Then what? After Blowtorch escaped? Would he hot-wire the prison van? Steal civilian clothes? Change his name and identity? And slip back into the community?

Jason felt his eyelids droop. He rested his head on the desk by the mouse pad. He only meant to stay there for a second, but suddenly everything—all the crazy things that had happened in the last few days—caught up with him.

He felt himself floating off to sleep. And he couldn't seem to resist. Sometime in the night his dad must've carried him to bed.

The next morning in the kitchen his parents were wearing wide grins. Cambria was there, too. She wore her favorite T-shirt: Play Always

Comes Before Work: Look It Up in the Dictionary. No knee or elbow pads. She must have left them outside with her skateboard.

Everyone wailed, "Happy birthday!"

Jason smiled back. "Thanks."

"How does it feel to be thirteen?" his dad asked, giving him a bear hug.

"Lucky thirteen!" his mom said, joining in on the squeeze.

"On leap year!" Cambria added.

Everyone settled around the kitchen table, digging into a platter piled high with strawberry waffles and sausage. *Real* sausage. Not the meatless kind his mom usually bought.

After breakfast his dad stacked the dishwasher. His mom disappeared from the room. "I'll be right back," she chimed.

She's going to get my presents, he thought excitedly.

Cambria wiped off the kitchen table. Sometimes she acted like a member of their family. More like a sister than a friend. Except they never bickered.

His mom returned, waving two red paisley handkerchiefs. The old-fashioned kind like the ones in Western movies. Jason tried not to show his disappointment. Maybe the presents were still hidden. Yeah, that was probably it. They'd appear later with cake and ice cream.

"Are you two ready?" his mom asked.

Jason and Cambria exchanged puzzled looks. "Ready?" they echoed.

His mom rolled the red handkerchiefs into blindfolds. "You said you wanted a surprise for your birthday."

"And that's what you're going to get!" added his dad.

I bet we're going to the circus, Jason thought. But he didn't say it out loud. He didn't want to ruin their surprise.

The blindfolds went quickly into place—pulled tight over their cheeks and knotted in back.

"No fair peeking," said his mom, leading the kids outside.

A few minutes later his dad helped them fasten their seat belts. "You guys all set?"

"Let's go!" said Jason.

His mom fired up the van and backed down the driveway.

Jason's thoughts turned to fire-eaters, sword-swallowers, and the motorcycle dude who sped across the high-wire. Plus all the wild animals: lions and tigers and elephants. He even pictured the dog acts—spotted police dogs driving miniature fire trucks with clowns squirting fire hoses.

Jason's stomach lurched every time the van made a sharp turn. He tried to remember the location of the circus. What did the poster say? Was the circus in the next town? The next county?

An hour later his mom said, "We're here, Fuzzy Wuzzy! You can take off your blindfolds now."

Fuzzy Wuzzy!

Jason yanked off the blindfold. He pressed his nose to the window and gaped at his surroundings. The word *no!* pounded through his thoughts. Was this another hallucination?

He rubbed his eyes. Maybe the blindfold had been tied too tightly.

"Surprise!" his parents sang out.

"Where are we?" Cambria asked, untying her blindfold.

Jason stared out the window at the state prison. Concrete block walls stared back, topped with shiny coils of barbed wire.

A three-story-high guard tower loomed over a city of moss-stained buildings.

A scar-faced prisoner glared down at him from one of the towers.

"Welcome!" Blowtorch called out.

Chapter

Jason gasped and scrambled out of the van. "No!"

Cambria was on his heels. "Is this a joke?" she said from behind him.

Blowtorch teetered menacingly on the guard tower. Below in the prison yard a gang of inmates with heavy chains around their ankles were using pickaxes to smash rocks.

"Thanks for helping me escape!" Blowtorch cackled above the din of ax blades striking granite. "Heating ducts! What an ingenious plan!"

"But I never put it in the computer," Jason sputtered back. "I was only thinking—"

Jason stopped short. *What am I doing? Trying to reason with a convicted murderer? A character that isn't even real?*

Or is he?

Jason grabbed Cambria by the hand and pulled her down the long prison driveway. Away from Blowtorch. Away from the prison. And away from his parents and the van.

Mom and Dad. He shuddered with dread. *Where are my real parents?*

The sun-soaked asphalt burned through the soles of his sneakers as he ran. Sweat dripped down his forehead and burned his eyes. His T-shirt was soaking wet.

"If Blowtorch used the end of my story to escape," Jason said, not missing a step, "where are the helicopters? The blinding spotlights? Why aren't sirens wailing?"

At least he thought he'd said it until he realized his throat had been sucked dry with fear and no sound had come out. He swallowed hard and decided not to try again until they reached the end of the driveway.

The next few moments were a blur as he raced past guard towers and chain-link fences topped with curls of barbed wire.

Finally at the end of the driveway, where the asphalt met the city street, Cambria yanked on his arm. "What's going on?" she cried, spinning him to a stop.

Now a safe distance from the guard tower, Jason glanced back at the two people who looked like his parents. They were standing next to the van like mannequins with fixed smiles. Somehow they'd instantly changed into the khaki prison uniform.

It was impossible. Blowtorch couldn't take over his parents.

It was as impossible as . . . as what? As his computer spitting sparks? As Mr. Glabrous making burritos in class? As Jason standing in front of a prison?

Jason shivered in sweat. Was *everything* really possible?

"I think it's . . ." Jason shook his head dully, and sweat flew off his brow. "I—I don't know."

"Jason!" his dad hollered. "Come back! We have your uniform. It's wrapped in a box with fluffy white tissue. And tied with a bright shiny ribbon. Mom even stitched your ID number over the pocket."

His mom beamed. "And I baked a cake with a file in it!"

Jason couldn't stop thinking about his real parents. What had Blowtorch done with them? Were they locked inside the prison in a cell? How could Jason—barely a teenager—break them out?

"Happy birthday to you!" the bogus pair sang.

"It's your story, isn't it?" Cambria muttered. "I'm so sorry, Jason. I should've believed you." Then she blinked at the city traffic. "Do you know where we are?"

"I don't know," he answered dismally.

Jason kept an eye on Blowtorch, who was now just a small figure on the top of the tower. Why wasn't Blowtorch chasing them? He could've stolen the family van by now.

No! Don't even think it! Jason suspected that his thoughts could fly from his brain into Blowtorch's twisted mind.

Cambria peered around. "I've never been in this part of town before."

Jason followed her gaze. The traffic was thick and speeding at eighty miles per hour down the highway. All the road signs had names like Lockup Lane and Turnkey Turnpike.

"I don't know where we are, either," he said. "But we have to get to my house. Back to my computer so we can rewrite the story. No . . . we have to destroy the disk."

Cambria stuck out her thumb. "Right."

"What are you doing?!"

"Hitchhiking."

"Are you crazy?" His voice cracked. "We can't hitchhike!"

"Why not?" she asked, still wagging her thumb.

"I'm not allowed to hitchhike. Besides, it's not safe." As soon as he said it he realized how stupid it sounded. "There has to be a bus stop around here somewhere."

Jason and Cambria hurried down the sidewalk with their arms linked together. Cambria led—Jason followed—facing backward. That way he could keep an eye on the prison driveway. If the van showed up, they'd duck behind a sign.

Every so often Jason stumbled off the curb. "Careful," said Cambria, pulling him up on the sidewalk. "You don't want to spend the rest of your birthday in the emergency room."

"Some birthday," he muttered.

The sidewalk seemed to stretch on forever, an endless concrete path. They passed sign after sign: Warden Way and Captive Court. Did everything in this part of town have prison names?

"Look!" Cambria said. "A bus stop!"

Jason spun around, facing forward. "Let's go!"

They raced full speed to the bus stop. Before

they had a chance to check out the schedule, a bus stopped at the curb. It coughed up a cloud of rusty fumes.

The door *whooshed!* open, and the kids scrambled up the steps. They stopped only to plunk coins in the meter.

Cambria rushed down the aisle. "Where is the bus going?" she asked.

"Who cares?" Jason said, sliding into the wide backseat. He mopped his sweaty brow on his T-shirt. The vinyl seat felt cool against the back of his calves. "Anywhere away from here is okay with me. Besides, we can change buses later."

Cambria brushed her damp curls off her forehead. "Right."

Jason peered out the bug-splattered window. Towering glass skyscrapers shared space with ultramodern domes. *That's odd,* he thought. *Prisons aren't built in the downtown district. And definitely not mixed in with fancy office buildings.*

While Jason considered the city's architecture, the bus let out another billow of exhaust and made a wide U-turn.

It was speeding back to the prison.

Chapter

11

"**W**hat's he doing?" Cambria's eyes widened in horror. "Where's he going?"

Jason stiffened in the seat, his gaze glued to the bus driver. Why hadn't he noticed this before? The driver was wearing khaki-colored pants and a pinstripe shirt. A lunch pail stood next to the gearshift. It probably held a sloppy bean burrito.

The bus crashed over the center divider in its U-turn. Cars in the other lanes slammed on their brakes and skidded. The smell of burning rubber poured in through the bus windows.

Jason clung to his seat to keep from being thrown onto the floor. His stomach pitched as the bus made another sudden turn. "Check out the driver!" he coughed through the toxic fumes.

Cambria's cheeks drained to the color of her gripping knuckles—bone white. "Oh, no!"

"We were in such a hurry to get off the street." Jason's voice shook in time with the bouncing tires. "We blew right by him."

"There's something else," she said. "We're the only passengers."

The driver let out a wild cackle. "Next stop, Jailhouse Rock." He threw back his head and laughed like a madman. "Get it?"

"What're we going to do?" Cambria sputtered.

"I don't know."

Jason peeked over the rows of empty seats, focusing on the back of the driver's head. A small mirror was hooked to the visor above the front window. The driver's reflection filled the mirror. A crusty scab covered his cheekbone. Just like the scab on Blowtorch's cheek.

Was Blowtorch cloning himself? Was he turning the city into one humongous prison? Would all the citizens become inmates? Blindly following his orders? *Mr. Blowtorch, City Father.* Jason shivered at the thought.

The bus driver flattened his lead boot on the accelerator, sending the speedometer spinning off the dial. All four of the bus's tires screamed in agony.

Quickly Jason scanned the windows. No, they weren't a safe escape route. The fall to the street would probably kill them. Or they'd be steamrollered by a car. The door? Yeah, it was the best bet. But how would they get past the driver?

Jason knew they couldn't stay where they were. Once the bus drove onto the prison grounds, they'd never escape. He felt it deep down in his gut. Then his eyes rested on a sign: Emergency Exit.

Just as the bus leaned into the final turn at the prison gate, Jason jumped up and kicked at the emergency door. "Ouch!" he wailed, stubbing his toe. Kicking was not the smartest choice for someone who barely passed PE.

A split second later Cambria joined him in kicking at the door.

"Get away from there!" the driver called back.

"One, two, three!" Jason said as they hammered the exit with their high-topped sneakers.

Bells and whistles exploded inside the bus as the emergency door finally flew open.

The bus skidded to a stop inches outside the

prison gate. "Come back here!" the bus driver hollered.

But Jason had already pushed through the exit.

"Where do you think you're going!" Blowtorch shouted.

"Jason, dear," his parents echoed. "We're waiting for you!"

But Jason didn't look back. He zigzagged through speeding traffic to the concrete island in the middle of the highway. Cars and trucks whizzed by on both sides. Horns honked and drivers shook their fists at him.

"Stupid kid!" shouted one senior citizen.

"What an ill-mannered brat!" someone else hollered.

"That younger generation!"

Jason doubled over, trying to catch his breath. *If they only knew!* "We made it, Cambria," he said. But when he turned around, Cambria wasn't behind him. "Cambria?"

The bus rumbled through the prison gate. Cambria was still on it!

Chapter

Jason stood shaking in his shoes on the raised concrete divider in the center of the highway. The divider gave him little protection from the stream of cars whizzing by.

Part of his brain was screaming, "Run, you idiot! Run!" Another part was shouting, "Follow that bus! You have to save Cambria!"

His legs ignored both sides—his knees just knocked together.

The bus had skidded to a wobbly stop at the prison gate. The emergency exit still flapped open. The door dangled lopsided on a bent hinge.

"Come on, Cambria!" Jason shouted over the blast of car horns. "The cars will stop for you.

This is California. Pedestrians have the right of way!"

Cambria's feet were running full blast. Her arms pumped as though she were in a marathon. But she wasn't going anywhere. She looked like a character on a Saturday morning cartoon.

Under other circumstances Jason might have laughed. But this wasn't funny. It was serious. *Deadly* serious.

The hem of Cambria's T-shirt was wrapped around the lever on the emergency door. "I'm stuck!" she shouted back.

In the distance, all the way down the asphalt driveway near the main prison buildings, Blowtorch loomed like a giant on the guard tower. He didn't say a word—which in a way was creepier than when he talked. He simply laughed, that same bloodcurdling laugh he'd tossed out earlier.

The background held two other figures: Mr. and Mrs. Robert A. Reed. They weren't talking, either. They just stood next to the family van in their matching prison uniforms.

They didn't holler at him, *Jason, what're you doing in the middle of the street?* Or, *Jason, go straight to the nearest crosswalk.* And no lilting voices sang, *Happy birthday to you!*

Of course not! Jason had to remind himself. *They're not real people!*

Now Jason watched in horror as the bus driver bounced down the steps. He was lumbering slowly and deliberately toward the rear of the bus, toward Cambria.

"Look out!" Jason warned his best friend. "The driver's coming after you!"

"What?" Cambria called, struggling like mad to free her shirt. "I can't hear you!"

"The bus driver!" But all his warnings were snuffed out by traffic sounds.

Then Jason noticed that the driver was carrying something under his arm. Was it his lunch pail? Jason wondered. Was he going to force a bean burrito down Cambria's throat? Is that how Blowtorch pulled people under his spell? Was that what had happened to Mr. Glabrous? And his parents?

Jason shuddered at another thought. *What would've happened to me if I'd eaten the burrito Mom fixed me as a snack?*

Jason stared wide-eyed as the bus driver closed in on Cambria. He wasn't carrying a lunch pail after all. It was a bundle of clothes.

Suddenly everything was silent. The traffic kept zooming by, but the tires were as quiet as shadows.

"Slip into these," the bus driver ordered Cambria. He shook out a pair of khaki pants and a pinstripe shirt. "Then you'll be free."

"No!" Jason shouted. He leapt into the oncoming traffic. A minivan zoomed straight at him. It didn't even swerve. "No!" he screamed again, jumping back onto the divider. Another second and he would've been an adolescent pancake.

Jason waited, holding his breath.

"What're you doing out there?" a familiar sugary voice oozed from behind. "You're gonna get killed!"

Jason would have recognized that candy-coated voice anywhere. He swiveled to the person standing on the sidewalk behind him. "B. B.?" he asked in astonishment.

Chapter

The next few seconds passed in a fuzzy haze.

B. B. stepped into traffic on her side of the street. Miraculously the cars stopped. She strolled to the center divider as if she owned it.

"What're you doing here?" she repeated.

"I have to get to that side of the street." Jason nodded toward Cambria and the bus. "And fast!"

The bus driver was helping Cambria untangle her T-shirt from the door handle. Was it his imagination? Or was there a weird glint in Cambria's eyes?

Cambria was nodding at the driver obediently, as if she was saying, "Thank you, sir." And she was holding the prison uniform.

"Don't put it on!" Jason shouted across the street.

"Don't put *what* on?" B. B. asked. "What's Cambria doing in front of the prison? How come that bus driver is wearing prison clothes?" Then she gasped, "Oh, my gosh! Is there a breakout or something? Is Cambria being held hostage? I knew I should've swiped Dad's cell phone when I was in his office!"

Jason stared at B. B. as if he'd never seen her before. Talk about an overactive imagination. What a minute. Just about everything B. B. had said was true. Cambria could be a hostage. Just like his parents.

"We have to get across the street before it's too late!" Then Jason did the single most unbelievable thing in the history of his thirteen-year life. He grabbed B. B. by the hand and pulled her across the street. "Let's go!"

B. B. fluttered her eyelashes and followed him blindly into the rushing traffic. Just as they had before, the cars skidded to a stop.

"How do you do that?" Jason asked, zigging across two lanes.

"What're they going to do? Hit me?" B. B. said, clinging tightly to his hand. But she wasn't holding on tightly because she was afraid. These were Jason Reed's fingers she was clinging to! "Everyone knows my dad's a lawyer. Right now he's in his office working on a million-dollar lawsuit."

Jason hopped the curb. "Right." He shook away B. B.'s grip. It wasn't easy.

Cambria was about to slip into the pinstripe shirt when Jason ripped it out of her hands. "No way!" he wailed.

"What's wrong with her?" B. B. asked.

"She's ours now, Jason," the bus driver croaked. "You might as well give up, too. And your pretty little friend here. What a nice addition she'll make to our community."

Jason shot a sideways glance at B. B., who he noticed for the first time was wearing mismatched clothes. Probably because it wasn't a school day. She almost looked like a normal seventh-grade kid.

Then she batted her eyelashes at the bus driver. "My name is Barbara Burton. And my dad's a prominent attorney in town."

"An attorney, eh?" The bus driver smacked his chops. "Blowtorch would probably give me a raise if I delivered a mouthpiece. Criminal or civil?"

"Just your average ambulance chaser," she

said, pointing at the towering skyscraper on the far side of the street. An impressive sign said Burton & Burton. Then she held out her hand for a how-do-you-do shake. "What's your name?"

"Don't touch him!" Jason warned, but he was too late.

The bus driver had already stuck out his hand. That's when B. B. bit his wrist. "Yeow!" the driver wailed. Next she kicked him in the shin. *Hard*. "You little brat!" he cried out.

Jason just stood there in shock while the driver retreated behind the bus.

"What did you think?" she shot at Jason. "That I had BBs for brains?"

Cambria suddenly snapped out of her trance. "Jason? What happened?" She blinked wildly. "B. B. What're you doing here?"

Jason turned at the sound of his parents' van revving its motor. But this time his dad wasn't behind the wheel. Blowtorch sat in the driver's seat. His meaty knuckles were on the gearshift, ready to yank it into drive. Something told Jason his phony parents were in the backseat.

"Run!" Jason shouted, then he took off down the busy street. Cambria and B. B. were right behind him.

Chapter

Jason led the trio running down the highway. His heart was racing as fast as his feet. If the school bus were breathing down his neck, he wouldn't have known it. The sound of his gasping breath filled his ears.

Don't look back! he kept telling himself. He concentrated on the sidewalk stretched out in front of him.

None of the three kids said a word for ten blocks. At the edge of Mockingbird Lane, the street Jason lived on, he ducked into a neighbor's hedge and scooted deep into the branches, making room for Cambria and B. B.

"This is kind of fun." B. B. crawled on her hands and knees behind Cambria. "What's going on, anyway?"

"You'd never believe it," Cambria said with a shiver. "Not in a zillion years."

"Try me," said B. B., and pushed a leafy twig away from her face.

Cambria sighed. Jason was sure she knew that if B. B. hadn't shown up when she did that she, Cambria Pines, would have become part of the burrito brigade. "You saved my life," she said. "Thank you."

"Yeah, thanks," Jason muttered. It didn't hurt too much to say it.

Jason and Cambria took turns spinning out the events of the last week. "Wow!" said B. B., her eyes wide in astonishment. "That explains the prison. It didn't used to be there."

"Really?" Cambria said.

"It's Blowtorch," Jason explained, looking even more worried. "He can do anything— anything he wants to."

Jason felt kind of good that B. B. believed the hair-raising story. But the feeling didn't last long. His own words, *Blowtorch can do anything he wants to,* echoed through his head. *Can Blowtorch be stopped?*

B. B. took the next words out of his mouth. "What now?"

The sound of squealing tires answered their

question. The kids pulled down a branch and squinted through the leaves.

"Oh, my gosh!" Cambria gasped.

B. B. shot, "Not him again!"

The bus rambled down the street. It was heading full steam ahead in their direction. "Come out! Come out! Wherever you are!" the bus driver pelted through a speaker stuck on the hood. "If you don't come out, you'll be *iiit!*"

Jason froze, afraid to breathe. He let his eyes make a thorough scan of the street. He expected to see the van, driven by Blowtorch. His parents as passengers. It worried him even more that the van wasn't in sight.

The bus pulled up at the curb, not twenty feet from the hedge. The door *whooshed!* open, and the driver limped on his sore shin down the steps. A gauze bandage covered his wrist where B. B. had bitten him.

"Burritos for sale!" he chimed as if he were selling hot dogs in a baseball stadium. "Get 'em while they're hot!"

Jason gulped what little spit he had left.

Across the street a lady darted from her house, purse in hand. Two little kids tugged on her skirt. *No!* Jason urged silently. *Don't buy any burritos!*

The bus driver counted out three bean burritos while his zombie eyes continued scanning the neighborhood. Then he stopped as still as a corpse and with those same lifeless eyes stared straight at the hedge.

No one moved.

No one breathed.

Even the wind stopped rustling the leaves.

The bus driver pulled a cellular phone from his hip pocket. After punching in some numbers he spat into the receiver, "They're not here, boss," and disappeared back inside the bus.

Jason and the girls breathed a sigh of relief when the bus was again rumbling down the street. It turned the corner, and B. B. whispered, "Maybe it's just a trick. Maybe he's not really leaving."

For the first time in three years Jason had to agree with her. "I'd bet my life on it."

Even Cambria was nodding. "But we have one advantage."

Jason tried to think of something. *Anything.* "What?" he asked.

"The bus driver? He's like a puppet," Cambria said. "Blowtorch is pulling his strings. We can still use our minds to figure things out. Besides, it's three against one."

B. B. nodded vigorously. "I always get an A-plus in math," she said proudly. "And those are excellent odds."

"What about Blowtorch? And my parents? And who knows how many other people?"

"Like Mr. Glabrous," Cambria suddenly remembered.

"But they're all programmed by the same person," B. B. said. "So it's still three against one."

Jason decided not to argue. What was the point? Besides, they needed some bit of hope. "Three against one," he said. Then he slapped high five with both girls.

The kids counted to one hundred before leaving the safety of the hedge. Cautiously they stepped into the sunlight, glancing in both directions. On tiptoes they crept to the sidewalk.

Jason knew he had to go back to his house and destroy the disk. That was all there was to it. But what if Blowtorch was waiting for him? And the bus driver?

No matter what B. B. said, those were deadly odds.

Chapter

15

Jason only hesitated a second. Then he took off down Mockingbird Lane, ducking into neighbors' yards every time he heard a car.

The bus never showed its ugly frame. Neither did the van. They all ran up the front walkway to his house. Jason barely slowed down as he snatched the key under the mat on the porch and burst into the living room.

Then it hit him: *What if they're inside? Waiting for us?*

"Let's go to my room." His voice was low and shaky.

Jason didn't really expect an answer. So he was startled when Cambria said, "We need to check out the house. Under the beds. In the closets. Uh, you know, just in case . . ."

B. B. closed her eyes and nodded. "Good plan."

Jason was back on tiptoes. Little pricks of fear ran up and down his spine. He took a couple of deep breaths, but it didn't seem to calm him. "Let's check out the kitchen first."

The trio moved slowly down the hall.

A floorboard creaked.

"Shhh!" Cambria tried to hush the squeaky floor.

Jason had lived in this house since he was a toddler. He had never heard the floors creak like this.

At the bathroom door B. B. let out a bloodcurdling scream. "Look!" B. B. paused and swallowed hard, seeming a little embarrassed at her outburst and terror-stricken at the same time.

The white porcelain sink was splattered with blood. A crisp white dress shirt lay in a crumpled heap on the floor.

"My dad . . . he cut himself shaving," Jason said shakily. "But that was days ago."

Cambria shook her head slowly. "I'm so sorry I didn't believe you, Jason. I should have. I mean, that's what best friends are for. But it all sounded so weird."

"We have much bigger problems now," B. B. tossed in. "Like getting rid of Blowtorch."

B. B. was right again.

A few seconds later the kids gathered in the kitchen. Everything seemed to be in order, neat and clean. Except that the kitchen table was set with metal plates and mugs and utensils with dull edges.

And all the ingredients for Blowtorch's burritos were lined up on the cutting board: beans, flour tortillas, Swiss cheese, and onions.

Jason shuddered in his sneakers. "They've been here."

"How long ago?" Cambria asked faintly.

B. B. spun around, staring at the door behind them. Then her eyes darted to the tall pantry door. "What if they're *still* here?" Her face paled to the color of the cheese.

Jason glanced at the pantry. It was big enough to hide one adult. Maybe two, if the cases of beans had been taken out. "What do you think?" Nervously he licked his lips. "It's now or never."

Cambria was by his side, trembling. "I'm ready."

Jason shuffled forward. "Okay. Let's go."

"No, wait!" B. B. cried.

Jason and Cambria swiveled to face her.

B. B. rushed over and threw her arms around Jason's neck. She squeezed him like he was a bottle of ketchup and she needed one last drop.

Jason shook her off. He was nervous enough without this yucky stuff.

Slowly he put his hand on the door and yanked it open.

Nothing.

The pantry was still filled with cases of beans.

Suddenly Jason heard the sound of tires crunching gravel in his driveway. All three kids rushed to the kitchen window and looked out.

Chapter

Jason's next-door neighbor climbed out of her car. Mrs. Applebaum's driveway was parallel to the Reeds' garage. Sometimes the noise made by her tires sounded like his parents' van.

Mrs. Applebaum was carrying a wiggling pillowcase. Jason knew a cat was inside. Relief washed over him. "She took Tiger to the vet again," he said. "And look—she's wearing normal clothes. No pinstripes."

Cambria turned away from the window. "We still have to check out the rest of the house."

Something in Jason's gut told him no one was there. Blowtorch had been in the house earlier. And his parents had probably been with him. But they'd all taken off. Jason called it gut instinct.

Where are they now? The thought flashed in and out of his head. The question that stuck was, *When will they be back?*

Still, the trio checked under beds and in closets and heaved enormous sighs when nothing popped out.

Now they gathered in Jason's bedroom. Jason glanced from Cambria to B. B. and back to Cambria. "We need a plan," he said in a low voice.

Cambria nodded grimly. "Before they come back."

"Maybe we can take the computer to the dump," B. B. said. "You know? Where your mom works?"

It bugged Jason that B. B. knew where his parents worked. She probably knew what he ate for breakfast every morning, too. "Okay," he said. "Then what?"

"Leave it there. Sooner or later the bulldozer covers everything. Puff! Now you see it. Now you don't. Buried under an avalanche of garbage!"

"Are you serious?" Cambria plopped down on Jason's unmade bed. She grabbed a pillow and hugged it. "That won't get rid of Blowtorch."

B. B. scrunched up her face. "Why not?" She sounded halfway ticked off. Then her expression softened. She must have realized it wouldn't be that easy to bury Blowtorch. "I guess you're right."

"What else?" Jason said. "Come on, let's think."

Suddenly Jason dropped into the chair at his desk and flipped on the computer.

B. B. looked at him uncertainly. "What're you doing?"

"I'm going to rewrite the story," Jason said. "Starting from the beginning."

"You already did that, remember?" Cambria joined B. B. at Jason's desk. "And Blowtorch changed it back."

"We have to try again," Jason insisted. His shoulders drooped as he clicked on the Pen Pal program. "Besides, I was trying to change the story before. I didn't change Blowtorch himself."

B. B. nodded. "Go for it."

Jason scrolled to the part of the story where he first described Blowtorch. Bloodshot eyes. Crusty scab. Food allergies: beans, onions, cheese.

Now Blowtorch stared back. Not in *words*. But an actual picture of the hair-dryer murderer filled the screen. His blubbery lips smashed against the glass. Then he laughed—that same bloodcurdling laugh they'd heard so many times before.

Jason's hand froze on the mouse.

Maybe this wasn't such a good idea after all.

Chapter

The chilling laugh echoed around the room. It bounced off posters and paperback books. Even Stephen King looked terror-stricken when the metal frame holding his picture started shaking. It shimmied right off the nightstand and crashed onto the floor. Broken glass pooled on the carpet.

Jason stared at the computer in horror. "W-What's going on?"

The sides of the computer started pulsing in and out. It spit out a steady *ka-boom! ka-boom!* that sounded like a blood-swishing heartbeat.

Jason gasped. "It's alive!"

Cambria gulped. "It has a heart!"

B. B. jumped back. "And a brain!"

Nothing but utter panic pushed Jason's fingers

across the keyboard. He typed like crazy, never looking at the ugly face smashed against the screen in front of him. The letters quickly covered the murderer's eyes, nose, and mouth.

Just as quickly the sides of the computer stopped heaving. With one last breath it belched. A small black bomb filled the screen.

Jason had never been so happy to see the bomb icon.

"You killed him!" Cambria shouted.

"I think you're right," he said, trying not to sound too cocky. Still, he did feel somewhat like a hero.

B. B. scooted closer, still shaking. "Are you sure?"

"Let's not take any chances," he said, restarting the computer.

Now B. B. looked on the verge of passing out.

Jason sucked in enough air to pop a bus tire and clicked on Pen Pal. Without opening the program, he dragged it to a blank disk and ejected it from the computer.

The floppy disk burned his fingertips. "Let's destroy it."

Cambria and B. B. nodded.

Jason darted from his bedroom to the laundry room. His mom kept small gardening tools in a cabinet under the sink. "Pruning shears," he said, snatching the rubber handles. The newly sharpened blades were blinding in their brightness.

Cambria's eyes widened. "Great idea!"

B. B. nervously twirled her long hair around her finger.

Jason was just about to slice the disk in half when the phone rang. All bodies did an about-face to the doorway.

"Should we answer it?" Cambria asked.

"Um, yeah," Jason said. "I mean, no."

Ring.

Cambria pressed him. "What do you think?"

Ring.

"Maybe we should let the machine get it," he said.

But the phone stopped on the third ring—one ring short of the answering machine switching on.

"We should've answered it." B. B. stared at the pruners. "It might've been someone who could've helped us."

"Yeah, maybe you're right. My grandparents always call on my birthday. It could've been them."

"Is today your birthday?" B. B. asked in surprise.

Jason nodded numbly. "Lucky thirteen."

"I would've gotten you a present," she said.

"Forget it." Jason didn't look at her. He had the uneasy feeling she was batting her eyelashes.

Then he held up the disk. In one quick movement he sliced the plastic into two jagged pieces. He handed one half to Cambria, the other to B. B. They took turns cutting their halves in two.

"I think we finally did it," Cambria said, looking relieved. Even her copper curls seemed to relax a little.

Jason took the snipped disk. "And just to make sure—" He pushed off down the hall to the kitchen and dropped the pieces in the trash compactor.

Cambria pressed *on*.

"Good riddance to bad rubbish," B.B. added over the crunching sound.

"No one can live through one hundred and fifty pounds of bone-crushing pressure," Cambria said. "Not even Blowtorch."

Jason should have felt happy. But he was suddenly overwhelmed with worry about his parents. *Where are they? Will I ever see them again?*

"What about my mom and dad?" he said slowly. "Where do you think they are?"

B. B. offered, "Maybe they're still at the prison." Now he was more worried than ever.

"No," Cambria assured him. "The prison wasn't real. You said so yourself. That it didn't even use to be there. It was something Blowtorch made up."

B. B. shook her head. "I still don't get it. How can a make-believe character come alive?"

Then Jason had another terrible thought. "What if I killed my parents? You know? What if they were in the disk? And I squashed them in the trash compactor?"

Jason staggered backward and collapsed into a kitchen chair. He didn't notice that the bottle of Bean-o still stood on the tablecloth.

Cambria joined him at the table. "That's impossible," she said. But her voice wasn't very convincing. "Blowtorch was made up. Your parents are real."

"Then where are they?" he asked again.

The phone rang.

"Maybe that's them now," B. B. offered in her cheeriest tone.

Jason didn't try to hide his excitement. He shot across the kitchen, skidding on the linoleum floor. "Hello?" he shouted into the cordless phone.

An all too familiar voice cackled into the receiver. "The trash compactor? Come on, kids! You can do better than that!"

Jason was so startled, the phone slipped from his hand.

"Did you really think you could get rid of me that easily?" Blowtorch laughed as the phone wobbled on the floor.

Chapter

18

Blowtorch's laugh was chopped off by a ten-point earthquake. The kitchen walls shook like gelatin. Even the linoleum floor rolled and wobbled, throwing the kids into cupboards and appliances. The bottle of Bean-o toppled off the table and crashed on the floor.

Jason clutched at the fridge, trying to get his balance. It took him several seconds to realize what had happened. It wasn't an earthquake at all. A vehicle had pulled into his driveway. But the tires now crunching across the gravel didn't belong to Mrs. Applebaum's car.

These tires could only belong to a big, heavy vehicle—like a bus.

Jason, Cambria, and B. B. rushed to the kitchen window. "Oh, no!"

On the other side of a window box stuffed with purple pansies stood the city bus. It let out a blast of exhaust and parked. The house stopped shaking.

Jason could see Blowtorch slouched behind the wheel, his grimy fingers clutching a microphone. The bus driver sprang up behind him, a gleam in his watery eyes.

Jason clenched the kitchen sponge, and drops of water squeezed out. "Our worst nightmare. It's coming true."

"And look," Cambria squeaked. "It's your parents!"

Jason followed her gaze. In the last seat his parents sat like statues with fixed unblinking stares. They wore the red paisley bandannas around their necks. The bandannas looked like they'd been tied too tightly.

Seeing his parents like that should have made him sad. And it did. But even more than that it made him mad. Fighting mad. Jason wrung the kitchen sponge as if it were Blowtorch's thick neck.

"Would you like to see your mommy and daddy?" Blowtorch's raspy voice filtered through the speaker on the bus hood. "Your *real* parents?"

Cambria stood next to Jason by the window. "Don't answer him," she warned. "He's just trying to get you out of the house."

B. B. agreed in a whisper. "It's a trick."

Jason didn't listen to them. Instead he flung open the window above the sink, all set to scream through the screen. But there wasn't any screen. His mom had taken it off so she could water the window box from inside.

For a moment Jason was startled, wondering if he should slam the window shut.

Then Blowtorch boomed through the microphone, "I have a proposition for you. A haggle-free deal." He giggled like a borderline case. "You in exchange for your parents. That's two for the price of one."

"It's a bargain!" the bus driver cackled. "You can't beat it!"

Jason looked Blowtorch straight in the eye. Of course the inmate was still inside the bus, so Jason had to squint through the bug-spattered windshield.

"What does he want me for?" Jason uttered in a low voice.

"I don't know," Cambria whispered back. "As it is, the creep does anything he wants to."

"Maybe you still have some power over him,"

B. B. said, shaking. "You know, like Dr. Frankenstein and the monster."

"Power?" Jason looked at B. B. Her hair was a mat of tangles, and the sleeve of her T-shirt had been torn. "Like what?" he asked.

Then it hit him like a ton of canned beans.

But before he could say anything, the bus door *whooshed* open. Blowtorch and the driver lumbered down the steps. "Think of it as a trade agreement." Blowtorch sneered. He now stood less than twenty feet from the open kitchen window. "It's a fair deal."

The bus driver smirked. "Even-steven."

Jason noticed Blowtorch had his hands behind his back. *He's holding something. What is it?*

Then Jason felt his knees start knocking. Rattat-tat.

What if it's a weapon?

Chapter 19

"**W**hat's the matter, kid?" Blowtorch lunged at the window, his hands still behind his back. "Don't you care what happens to your mommy and daddy?"

The words slapped Jason across the face. "You're nothing but a bully!" he spit out. "And you're ugly. Just like *your* mother!"

"Shhh! Jason!" Cambria tugged on Jason's sleeve. "You're going to make him even madder."

B. B. tugged on the other side. "Ditto!"

Jason shook them off. "And your mother wears combat boots!" he said in his best *so there!* tone.

Blowtorch's face was always red, a ruddy color

with spidery veins. Now his cheeks puffed like an overripe tomato—the skin shiny and stretched—ready to burst.

Blowtorch planted his feet in the flower bed. He swung the pink hair dryer out from behind his back. Then he aimed it at Jason. "Come out!" he ordered, sneering. "Or I'll let you have it between the eyes."

"A hair dryer?" Jason's voice peaked. "That's the murder weapon in my story!"

Cambria sucked in a breath. "Murder weapon?"

B. B. looked perplexed. "A hair dryer?"

Jason didn't answer them. He deserted his post at the kitchen sink and raced to the pantry. Then he filled his arms with canned beans. Chili beans. Racing back to the window, he started firing the cans at Blowtorch. *Boom, boom, boom.*

"Ouch! That hurts!" Blowtorch cried, then he shouted at the driver, "Get those kids! All three of them! Now!"

Jason threw the rest of the eight-ounce cans in rapid fire. *Bam, bam, bam.* One can clinked on the bus hood. Another one bonked the bus driver on his noggin. "Ow!" he squealed, and retreated to the bus.

Cambria ran back and forth from the pantry,

keeping Jason supplied with cans. "Go to the vegetable drawer in the fridge!" he called to B. B. "Get the onions!"

In a split second B. B. rushed back with a bunch of onions. "You want me to throw them?" she asked excitedly. All traces of fear had left her voice, too. "I'm a pretty good shot—I always get an A-plus in PE."

"Dump them in the trash compactor," he said quickly, not taking his eyes off Blowtorch. He was holding the hair dryer cord, looking for a place to plug it in.

"What're you going to do?" Jason hollered. "Fluff me to death?"

Jason noticed the electrical outlet on the outside wall of the garage. It was above the garden hose. *Water and electricity,* he thought. *That's how Blowtorch killed his last victim.*

Even though Jason was in the house and Blowtorch was outside, Jason figured the odds were pretty good that (1) Blowtorch could climb through the window and/or (2) somehow zap him with the hair dryer and hose at the same time.

B. B. broke into his thoughts. "You want the onions in the trash compactor?" she repeated.

"That's what I said!" he blurted, not taking the time to explain. "And hurry!"

B. B. dumped the onions in the compactor. As soon as she hit the *on* switch the aroma of smashed onions filled the kitchen.

Jason reached for a tea towel and blotted his burning eyes.

Cambria wiped her runny nose on her shirtsleeve.

B. B. sneezed, and the onion cloud swirled out the window.

Blowtorch stumbled backward, batting at the toxic fumes. "Not onions!" he wailed. "Anything but onions!"

"Get the Swiss cheese!" Jason told Cambria. "Rub it all over the computer! Smush it in the disk slot! And don't forget to cream the printer!"

Cambria didn't even question it. She just grabbed the block of cheese and vanished down the hall toward Jason's bedroom.

Jason kept pelting Blowtorch with canned beans. "Take that!" he wailed. "And that!"

One of the cans skidded at Blowtorch's feet. It busted wide open. Just the smell of beans triggered Blowtorch's allergies. His head inflated like a beach ball. His body swelled like the Goodyear blimp. He bobbed lightly from one boot to the other, as if a puff of wind could blow him away.

"Not beans!" Blowtorch cried in agony. "I'm allergic to the little brown boogers!"

"I should know," Jason said, now armed with a can opener. "I gave you the allergies."

B. B. helped Jason open the cans. "I'll get a couple of spoons," she said eagerly.

Jason and B. B. leaned over the sink and flung brown globs out the window. *Splat!* The first glob spattered Blowtorch's pinstripe shirt. Blowtorch started to float. *Splat!* The next shot hit him between the eyes. Blowtorch left the ground, bouncing up onto the bus hood. *Splat!* Now he hovered above the antenna.

A breeze whipped up and blew Blowtorch in a furious circle. "Help!" he called out. "I'm getting dizzy!"

"Beans, beans, the musical fruit," Jason shouted through the window. "The more you eat, the more you toot!"

Jason, Cambria, and B. B. watched in utter amazement as Blowtorch bounced one, two, three times on the pointy antenna. Even he, Jason Reed, writer of scary stories and author of "Blowtorch Burns Buns," could not have predicted what was about to happen.

Chapter

Blowtorch bounced one last time on the antenna. *Ka-boom!* The antenna tore a gaping hole in the blimp. Blowtorch buzzed like a burst balloon, zigzagging all over the neighborhood. He finally fell in a deflated lump in front of the bus. His body was shriveled down to the size of a single chili bean.

Blowtorch had burped his last belch.

The bus driver lumbered down the steps, a mere shadow of his former self. In an instant he evaporated into thin air.

"The end," Jason said solemnly.

Cambria and B. B. huddled next to him at the sink, looking out the window. "I can't believe it's really over," Cambria said.

B. B. nodded. "You can say that again."

And they did. "It's over!"

The bus started withering up like someone had let the air out of its tires. It shriveled to the size of the Reeds' family van. Then it stopped shrinking. Right before three pairs of disbelieving eyes, the van started up and drove into the garage.

The kids uttered, "Wow!"

A moment later Mr. and Mrs. Reed stepped into the sunshine. They smiled just like always and waved. "Hi, kids!"

Jason rushed out the back door and ran down the porch steps. He threw his arms around his parents and hugged them like the long-lost relatives that they were.

"Mom! Dad!" Jason was on the verge of tears. "It's you! It's really you!" His parents hugged him back. Nothing had ever felt so good in his whole life. "You're back for good," he said with another back-breaking squeeze.

His mom stepped away with a puzzled expression. "Back? We only drove into town." Then she said, "Are you ready for your birthday surprise?"

"We have something special planned," his dad said, following them up the porch steps. "Extra special."

Inside, Cambria and B. B. had cleaned up most of the mess in the kitchen.

Cambria held the broom behind her back. "Hi, Mrs. Reed," she said. "Mr. Reed."

"Hi!" said B. B.

"Cambria! B. B.!" his mom said. "I'm so glad you're both here. Now call your parents. Let them know you'll be gone the rest of the day. We have something planned for Jason's birthday. He's thirteen today, did you know that?"

"Lucky thirteen!" his dad added.

Jason groaned, embarrassed by all the attention. Besides, he'd had enough surprises to fill a lifetime. "Gone for the day?" he asked. "Where are we going?"

"Now, son." His dad draped an arm over his son's shoulders. "If we told you, it wouldn't be a surprise. Would it?"

Jason looked into his dad's eyes. He didn't want to hurt his parents' feelings. Especially after what they'd been through. Still, he could not—under any circumstances—climb back inside the van. Not today. Maybe not ever.

Maybe it sounds lame, he thought. *But I want to stay home with my friends. That would be the best birthday present of all.* And that's what he told his mom and dad. They both looked at him as if they thought he'd lost his marbles. But they finally agreed.

"I'll drive over to the bakery," his mom said. "And pick up the cake."

"I'll get the ice cream from the freezer in the garage," said his dad, following his wife out the door.

Cambria smiled at Jason. "Guess we'd better clean up your computer," she said. "It's covered with Swiss cheese. And so is the printer."

The two of them started toward his bedroom. At the doorway Jason stopped and looked back.

B. B. just stood in the hall. Her blond hair was still a matted mess. Only now it was streaked with bean juice. "Aren't you coming?" he asked.

B. B. shrugged. "Do you want me to?"

At least she didn't make gooey eyes at him. "Sure," he said. "Come on."

B. B. smiled and followed along.

The inside of Jason's room looked like a tornado had struck. Papers were scattered everywhere. Books had fallen off the shelves. And the computer and printer were covered with globs of Swiss cheese.

Jason picked up his yellow pad and scanned the notes for his short story. "I wonder if I have time to write another story," he said. "Before the deadline of the contest."

Cambria and B. B. exchanged looks. "*Not!*"

Jason wadded his notes and tossed them in the waste can. "Just kidding."

Thank goodness I won't have another "leap" birthday for four more years, he thought with a smile.

ABOUT THE AUTHOR

Betsy Haynes has written over fifty books for children, including *The Great Mom Swap*, the bestselling The Fabulous Five series, and the Taffy Sinclair books. *Taffy Goes to Hollywood* received the Phantom's Choice Award for Best Juvenile Series book of 1990.

When she isn't writing, Betsy loves to travel, and she and her husband, Jim, spend as much time as possible aboard their boat, *Nut & Honey*. Betsy and her husband live on Marco Island, Florida, and have two grown children, two dogs, and a black cat with extra toes.